Animal Babies

Ducklings

by Meg Gaertner

FOCUS READERS

SCOUT

www.focusreaders.com

Focus Readers is distributed by North Star Editions:
sales@northstareditions.com | 888-417-0195

Produced for Focus Readers by Red Line Editorial.

Photographs ©: PatiharnPaeJar/Shutterstock Images, cover, 1; Vladimir Zabegaylov/iStockphoto, 4, 16 (top left); lissart/iStockphoto, 7, 16 (top right); Inna G/Shutterstock Images, 9 (top); shaftinaction/Shutterstock Images, 9 (bottom), 16 (bottom left); ElenaGwynne/Shutterstock Images, 11; Guido Bissattini/Shutterstock Images, 13, 16 (bottom right); Olga Enger/Shutterstock Images, 15

Library of Congress Cataloging-in-Publication Data
Names: Gaertner, Meg, author.
Title: Ducklings / by Meg Gaertner.
Description: Lake Elmo, MN : Focus Readers, [2020] | Series: Animal babies | Audience: K to Grade 3. | Includes index.
Identifiers: LCCN 2018056930 (print) | LCCN 2018058975 (ebook) | ISBN 9781641859523 (PDF) | ISBN 9781641858830 (ebook) | ISBN 9781641857451 (hardcover) | ISBN 9781641858144 (paperback)
Subjects: LCSH: Ducklings--Juvenile literature.
Classification: LCC QL696.A52 (ebook) | LCC QL696.A52 G335 2020 (print) | DDC 598.4/11392--dc23
LC record available at https://lccn.loc.gov/2018056930

Printed in the United States of America
Mankato, MN
May, 2019

About the Author

Meg Gaertner is a children's book editor and author. She lives in Minneapolis, Minnesota. When not writing, she is usually dancing or spending time outside.

Table of Contents

egg
feathers

First Days

Ducklings are baby ducks.
They hatch from eggs.
They are wet.
They have **feathers**.

Ducklings stay in
a **nest**.
They dry off.
Their mother keeps
them warm.

mother
nest

Changes

Ducklings get older.

They follow their mother.

They swim.

They eat **grass** and seeds.

grass

Ducklings lose
their feathers.
They grow new ones.

Ducklings grow fast.

Their **wings** get strong.

They fly.

wing

Growing Up

Ducklings keep growing.
They leave their mother.
They live in groups.

Glossary

feathers

nest

grass

wings

Index